HarperFestival is an imprint of HarperCollins Publishers.

Plants vs. Zombies: Brains and the Beanstalk
Text and illustrations copyright © 2013 by Electronic Arts Inc.
Plants vs. Zombies is a trademark of Electronic Arts Inc.

Library of Congress catalog card number: 2012956503
ISBN 978-0-06-222836-9

Typography by Rick Farley
14 15 16 17   CWM   10 9 8 7 6 5 4
❖
First Edition

Brains and the Beanstalk

By Annie Auerbach and PopCap Games
Illustrated by Charles Grosvenor and Jeremy Roberts

An Imprint of HarperCollinsPublishers

Once upon a time, in a peaceful village, Jack and his mother received a strange note in the mail.

"I always thought we'd have a fairy tale ending," Jack's mother
cried. "What'll we do now?"

Jack looked out the window at his lawn, which was lined with old
lawn mowers. He saw the zombies approaching far off in the distance.
"Does this mean I don't have to fix those old lawn mowers?"

"That's it!" said Jack's mother. "Go and sell our best lawn mower and buy something to save us!"

Jack didn't know which one to choose, so he quickly grabbed the least-ugly lawn mower and hurried away.

On the way to the market, Jack met a bearded man who smelled a bit odd and was selling things out of his car.

"Hi, there! I'm Crazy Dave. But you can call me Crazy Dave!"

Jack was nervous. "Sorry, no time for crazy! I need help to fight zombies and all I have is this old lawn mower."

"Zombies! My favorite. I just talked to a puppet!" Crazy Dave smiled, and Jack was confused. "I have everything you need," Crazy Dave continued, and he showed Jack a packet of seeds that sparkled in the sunlight.

Jack couldn't resist, and he quickly made the trade.

When Jack returned home, his mother was furious. "What? Magic seeds?" she bellowed. "What good are those against the zombies?" She threw the seeds out the window in disgust.

But the seeds really were magic. And fast, too! In an instant, up from the ground rose a gigantic beanstalk.

Jack couldn't believe his eyes. The huge plant stretched far up into the sky, disappearing into the clouds. "It's amazing," he said. "I just wish it was made of pizza!"

Jack went outside to take a closer look at the beanstalk. Just then, the zombies arrived.

"Brains . . ." they mumbled.

"Oh no!" said Jack. His mother yelled for him to come inside, but he was surrounded.

Then Jack saw that the enormous plant was actually made up of hundreds of Peashooters. And they were pelting the zombies with peas. "Woohoo!" Jack said. "Mom, I finally like peas!"

But there were A LOT of zombies. Too many for the Peashooters to fight. Jack had nowhere to go but up. So he started to climb.

At the top of the beanstalk, Jack arrived at a land floating on clouds. And best of all: no zombies! He quickly made his way toward a majestic castle he saw looming in the distance.

Just outside the castle walls, Jack made an amazing discovery: a beautiful Marigold planted in the garden. It produced silver and gold coins!

"What a treasure!" Jack dug up the Marigold and danced with glee. "My mom and I will be rich!"

Suddenly the ground shook. The Marigold shivered in fright. A voice boomed, "Bree! Bri! Bro! BRAINS!"

And Jack remembered the zombies. "Uh-oh. This can't be good," said Jack.

It wasn't even half good. In front of him stood a Gargantuar–a gigantic zombie! And on his back, a tiny Imp Zombie. It was weird . . . and terrifying . . . and really weird!

"Brains!" said the zombie.

"But I'm just a small boy," said Jack. "I only have a tiny brain."

"Mmm . . . brains," said the zombie.

Jack grabbed the Marigold and ran through the enormous garden. But the hungry Gargantuar was getting closer and closer.

Jack spied a huge pile of magic seeds by a rock. He grabbed the Winter Melon and Spikeweed seeds and quickly planted them.

"Watch your step!" Jack said, and he laughed as the Spikeweed pricked Gargantuar's toes.

But still, Gargantuar kept approaching.

Jack planted Peashooters, Squash, and even Garlic. He held his nose. "Eew, it stinks like bad breath!"

Gargantuar took a club and raised it over his head. Down came the club, clobbering the plants.

Jack knew he was next to be smashed!

Jack had one more idea: Jalapeños. But he only had two. If his planting wasn't perfect, Jack was doomed. "No time for pepperation," Jack said. He took a deep breath and started digging.

"How about we spice things up!" Jack lured the Gargantuar closer and closer. The Jalapeños began to bubble and boil. Then, all of a sudden . . . BOOM!

The Gargantuar flew through the air and plummeted toward the earth below.

SMASH! The Gargantuar landed on all the zombies in the village, and squished them flat!

Jack climbed down the giant beanstalk, proudly carrying the Marigold. His mother cheered and hugged Jack.

"I'm so proud of you," Jack's mother said. Now that all the zombies were gone, their village was peaceful again. And Jack and his mother lived happily ever after.

With a giant zombie-zapping plant in their backyard.